# ZOMBIE'S INBOUND

## THE COLLAPSE OF MANKIND

### JEREMIAH BREUER

**MILTON & HUGO L.L.C.**
4407 Park Ave., Suite 5
Union City, NJ 07087, USA

**Website:** *www. miltonandhugo.com*
**Hotline:** *1- 888-778-0033*
**Email:** *info@miltonandhugo.com*

Ordering Information:
Quantity sales. Special discounts are available on quantity purchases by corporations, associations, and others. For details, contact the publisher at the address above.

Library of Congress Control Number:    2024911730
ISBN-13:          979-8-89285-133-6     [Paperback Edition]
                  979-8-89285-132-9     [Digital Edition]

Rev. date: 06/10/2024

# CHAPTER 1

# THE BEGINNING

It was a rough start to the day. Last night, my friends invited me to go get some drinks, but I didn't drink. However, I don't want to miss a good night, so I told them I would just hang out. We went to Mack's Bar and Grill down the street from me. I really don't know what happened because it's one in the morning and I was plastered. I couldn't remember what all happened or how I even got here, so I thought it was a good time to go home. I went outside and got in my truck and proceeded to somewhat drive home. A police officer turned on his lights, and I thought I was done for. But he flew right past me. I was freaking out. I pulled over and took a deep breath. I made it home and went to bed. The next morning, I had a massive headache. I went downstairs and took some medicine and turned on the news. I sat on the love seat and passed out. About an hour later, I woke up to my neighbor screaming. They were always fighting with each other but not really this early in the morning. I looked at my phone, and it was completely dead. I plugged my phone in and went to get dressed. I came back down, and my phone had enough charge to turn on. I turned my phone on, and I had fifty-two text messages and a ton of missed calls from my mother. She lived about three hours from me. It must have been important if she called and texted that much. I called her back, and she picked up on the first ring. I said, "Mom, what's wrong? Is everything okay?

She was stuttering really badly. She said, "It's your father, he's very ill."

My mom started to cry and I told her, "Hang on, Mom I'm on my way, I'll see you soon." I grabbed my keys and drove for what seemed like forever. I finally made it to my parents' house. When I got to the door, I knocked, and my mom opened the door.

"Hurry, come quick! He's lying on the bed," she told me. When I got to his room, my dad was bleeding from his eyes and nose, and then he coughed blood everywhere. I looked at my mother and asked her, "Did you call 911?"

She said, "Yes! I did, and they said they can't do anything because they're too busy and they hung up on me."

I thought that was crazy, so I called them myself. The phone went to a presidential alert, and it said, "Please stay indoors. Block all the windows and barricade the doors. Emergency services are doing all that they can. This is not a test. I repeat, this is not a test. May God help us all!" Then the phone went out.

# CHAPTER 2

# DEATH

My mother screamed, "He's not breathing!" I dropped my phone and ran to his room. I saw my dad dead on the bed, not breathing. My mother was sobbing. I grabbed her hand and pulled her off Dad and close to me, and I hugged her. I asked, "Where's Dad's gun?" She looked at me, sobbing. She said, "He keeps that stupid thing in the safe." She pointed under the bed, and I found the safe. I asked my mom what the code was. She said, "It's your birthday, 03-15." I opened the safe, and there it was, my dad's M1911 and a box of ammo, but next to the box was a box of 5.56mm, which means my dad has an AR that my mother didn't know about. I asked, "Did you know Dad had an AR?"

She looked at me, confused, and said, "He might, I don't really know." I asked if she could look for it, and she left and went downstairs. While she was gone, I filled the M1911 up all the way, eighteen rounds. My mother yelled out loud, "I found it!" I walked to the basement stairs, and she was holding the AR with an extra mag. She handed me the gun and said I could keep it. My mother went back to the room to see my dad, and then she screamed, "He's alive! He's alive! I saw his finger move!"

I rushed back to my parents' room where my mother was hovering over my dad's body. Then I saw it too. His finger moved. I smiled and started to walk closer to them, then Dad's eyes opened, and he lunged and dug his teeth into my mom's neck. She was bleeding everywhere. I dropped the AR and pulled out the pistol, and I shot my dad in the chest, but he kept going after my mom. I finally pointed the gun again and shot him in the head. He went down like a sack of potatoes. I rushed over to my mom to try to stop the bleeding, but she was already dead. Before I could cry or feel anything, there was a knock on the door. It honestly scared me, then it got louder and louder. I walked to the front door with the M1911 in my hand ready for whatever was going to happen. I opened the door, and it was Karen, Mom's friend. She had blood all over. She said, "Help!" But before I could say anything, her head exploded. Blood and brains went everywhere. Her body dropped to the ground, and behind her was her husband, Frank, with a smoking barrel. He asked if I was bit. I said, "No, I'm not bit, what's going on?"

He said, "It's the zombie apocalypse."

# CHAPTER 3

# ZOMBIES?

Frank looked at me and asked, "Where are your parents?"

I said, "My dad died and came back to life and bit my mom. I had to shoot him. I shot him in the chest, but he kept going after her, so I had to shoot him in the head."

Frank looked at me with fear in his eyes and said, "Did you shoot your mom in the head too?"

"No, Frank, I did not shoot my mom in the head." Frank raised his gun and pointed it at me, and he took a shot. The bullet went past me and hit my mom that was right behind me, about to kill me. He told me, "When one gets bit, they turn."

I was dumbfounded. I turned and grabbed the AR and started to load it. Frank yelled at me, "Come on! Grab what you can and let's go." I came back out and asked him where we were going.

"The gun shop, for more ammo and guns and then to the store to get some supplies then to my cabin."

I grabbed my keys, and we left. We arrived at the gun shop, but it was being looted as we speak, so Frank gave me a duffel bag and told me to fill it with whatever I could find. And we went in. One guy shot another guy for taking his ammo out of his bag. When we left the gun shop, there were a few people on the ground. It looked like they were eating a person. I pulled out my gun, but Frank put his hand on the gun and pushed it down. He told me to save the ammo, plus they would all come if they heard the gunshot. He pulled out a knife and asked me if I had one. "Of course." I went into my pocket, but I remembered I left it at my house. "No, Frank, I don't have a knife, but wait, I have an ax in my truck." I walked to my truck and grabbed my ax, and we killed the people on the ground eating that guy. Then Frank stabbed the guy the others were eating in the head. "Just to be safe," he said. We made it out of there and went to the store. The store was packed full of people, but we didn't know if there were zombies or not. It looked like they were human.

We got out of the truck and were about to walk in, but then I thought, *What if someone was to steal the truck?* I told Frank I'd stay and watch the truck. He agreed and said, "Don't leave me," and he disappeared into the store.

# CHAPTER 4

# OTHERS

Few minutes went by and a man came out pushing people. I saw his eyes, and they were bloody. We locked eyes, and I raised up my AR, and he raised his pistol and—*BANG!* My gun went off, and the man dropped to the ground. I was shaking because that was technically the first person I killed, and it didn't feel right. I looked down at the front of the store and I saw a man on the ground, shaking like he was having a seizure. I pointed my gun at him, but before I could shoot him, something grabbed my foot. I freaked out and pointed my AR down, and it was a young girl like ten or eleven. She asked if I could help her. When I looked back up, that man went into the store where Frank was. About two minutes later, I heard three gunshots go off, and the first thing I thought of was I hope Frank was okay, then he walked out of the store, pushing a shopping cart full of supplies with a fat smile on his face. When he made it back to my truck, he saw the girl, and that smile went away. Before I could say anything, he said, "No, no, no, we are not helping this thing. She's going to slow us down."

I looked back at Frank and said, "At least let's take her out of the city so she doesn't get hurt."

Frank got done loading the supplies into the truck and said, "Fine, we'll help her get in the truck." She jumped in the truck, and then we left. As we were leaving, we heard screams then more gunshots. I was glad we got there when we did. Frank looked at me then at the girl. "What's your name, girl?"

The girl said, "My name is Carly. What are your names?"

Frank looked at me, and I said, "I'm Denver, and this is Frank."

Frank yelled at me, "You fool! You don't use your real names!" And he pouted then went back to driving the truck, not talking. Carly then asked where we were going. I didn't say anything because I didn't know if he'd get mad, but then he said, "We're going to my cabin. It's small, but it has a bunker. And we can call it home for a few weeks to see if this zombie thing dies down or if they can find a cure."

Carly looked at me and said, "Can I please stay with you guys?"

Before I could say yes, Frank licked his lips and said, "Yeah, you can stay with me...I mean you can stay with us."

That made me a little worried because I didn't really know this guy. We drove until my truck ran out of gas.

"We almost made it. The cabin is less than a mile away," Frank said. We hopped out of the truck and gathered the supplies, then Frank saw a beat-up car that still could run. He broke the window, and the alarm went off. Frank hurried and popped the hood and disconnected the alarm to the car. The alarm stopped, but then a deep voice said, "WHAT ARE YOU DOING!" It freaked us out really bad, but when I turned around, it was a man on a beautiful white horse. Frank stopped what he was doing and said, "We locked our keys in the car, that's all. Just mind your own business."

The man said, "I have never seen you folks around here before. Where are you heading?" I opened my mouth and said, "A cabin just up—" Then Frank cut me off and said, "Just up a few miles from here." The man saw all the guns we had and asked if he could have one or two to protect his ranch. I know we had more than enough, so I grabbed an AR and a few boxes of ammo and handed it to the guy. Then Frank punched me hard in the gut. "Stupid boy, don't give away my guns," he said. I got so mad I said, "Your guns? I helped get them too, so it's like fifty-fifty."

Frank pulled his pistol and shot the man on the horse. The gun and ammo fell to the ground. The horse ran away, dropping the man on the ground. He held his chest and then he died right in front of Carly and me. Carly and I both had a scared face and we whispered to each other as Frank went to retrieve the gun and ammo. We both said he needed to be stopped.

# CHAPTER 5

# THE PLAN

We got the car running, and we drove the rest of the way to his cabin. Carly and I unpacked the truck, and Frank opened the door. When we went inside, it was actually very nice. There were deer heads on the wall. It was not as creepy as I thought it might be. Frank walked over to a bookshelf and pulled a book down, which opened a door behind it. It led to a staircase going down to the bunker. I walked over, and we went down into the bunker. There were guns upon guns down there. I got really mad.

"Really, Frank? You have all these guns and you couldn't give that man one gun?"

Frank told me, "The more guns you have, the longer you will survive in this world."

I saw Carly, and we locked eyes. She grabbed a small handgun and put it in her pocket. I had my dad's M1911 and the AR. Frank was not getting these. It was getting dark out, so Frank told us to turn off all the lights. It was now pitch-black outside, and we used small flashlights in between our fingers so no outsiders could see in. Frank gave his room to me to sleep in, and Carly got the guest room. Frank said he'd sleep on the couch. It was now about one in the morning, and Carly came to my room and said that we needed to stop him before he killed one or both of us. So that night, we made a plan to get rid of him. We thought about cutting his neck or stabbing him, but with his knowledge, he might know how to survive. We didn't come up with a good plan sooner, but eventually we did. It was now three in the morning, and Carly was passed out on my bed. I picked her up and took her to her room and laid her down on her bed and tucked her in. I went back to my room, and I fell asleep.

The morning came, and when I woke up, I went to check on Carly. I got to her room, and the door was open. I knocked, but she didn't answer. I went in, and she was gone. I went downstairs, and Frank was gone too. I didn't think much of it, but then Carly screamed. I grabbed the gun by the front door, and I went outside. I saw Carly running with wood in her hands and Frank fighting off a bunch of zombies. I thought, *Now's the chance to take him out.* But then I wouldn't be able to get into the bunker. The bunker had a code on it. As soon as I get the code, that's when I'd kill him. I shot the gun—*BANG! BANG! BANG!* I went through a whole mag. I killed at least twenty to thirty zombies. It was crazy. Carly ran behind me and said, "He's the reason they're all dead. He's a monster."

Moments later, Frank walked over to me and said, "Thanks. I wouldn't have been able to take them all on my own." Then Frank turned around and started dragging the bodies and put them in a pile. He stopped and looked at me and he said, "Well, are you just going to stand there or are you going to help me so we can burn them?"

"Yeah," I said. "Let me use the can right quick," and I went inside. I went to Carly's room where she was on the bed, crying. "Carly, what happened?"

"Well, we went out this morning to get some firewood, and we ran into a group of people who built a camp. Frank shot a guy, yelling for them to get off his property. When they didn't move, he shot all of them, killing them."

"Okay, Carly, I'll kill him tonight."

Carly cut me off and said, "No, I'm killing him. He tried to touch me this morning. When she said that, I got super angry. How should we do it?" Carly said.

"Well, we wait till night when he's asleep, and we shoot him in the head." We both agreed and we went on about our day. We had a few more zombies stroll by, but we took care of them. It soon became nightfall, and it was now time. Time to kill Frank!

# CHAPTER 6

# THE WORST DAY OF OUR LIVES

It was about three in the morning when Carly and I started our plan. We went downstairs to see Frank sitting on the couch, not sleeping. He was just sitting there. It was kinda freaky to be honest. Carly raised her gun and pointed it at Frank. Frank turned around, and his eyes were bloody. Frank was a zombie. He got up and started to rush toward me when Carly shot him, dropping him to the floor. Blood went everywhere.

"We need to go," I told Carly. We headed to the bunker where the door was left open and all the guns and ammo were gone and the room was empty save for a small box with a note on it. We both turned around, and the door shut and locked. Carly and I were trapped. I walked to the door and I tried opening it, but it would not open. I heard an explosion, and the door got super hot. Carly went to the box and opened it. It had some water bottles and MREs in it. MREs are meals ready to eat. The note said, "I'm sorry, I did what I had to do. I took all the guns and ammo, and I buried them on the property. If you're in this room and the door is locked and you feel heat, it's because the cabin is burning down. I had a self-destruct on this cabin so no one can use the cabin. The doors will open in forty-eight hours."

Carly and I looked at each other. We didn't have a sense of time down there. There was a small air vent where we could see the sky. It was bright, but it was still nighttime. It was the cabin burning down. We could hear the moaning of zombies walking around and the fire crackling. We lay down on the floor and went to sleep. The next morning, we woke up, and we had nothing to use for a bathroom. So what we did was we flipped some tables around and made a small room so we could use it as bathroom. A few hours went by and we heard a loud crash. The door to the bunker broke, and it opened. We went outside and saw a dual-prop plane on fire. We made it out of the ashes. But then we heard more moaning. We looked around, and just through the smoke were hundreds of zombies. We only had three guns: my AR15 and M1911 and Carly's small gun. Definitely not enough ammo to take them all on. We were looking around for a way out. Carly spotted a few bikes. We ran to the bikes, but only one worked. I put her on the bike and told her to go, go, go. She didn't move. She said, "If you die, I will die too." So I picked her up and put her on my back. I jumped onto the bike, and we left. I pedaled and pedaled until I got tired. There was a sign saying that there was a small town just up the road. I got off the bike and looked behind us. The zombies were still coming, but they were still a long ways away. I got off the bike, and I let Carly ride the bike to the town. I walked. We eventually made it to the town.

# CHAPTER 7

# THE TOWN

The town was very small; it had one gas station and three family-owned stores. Carly asked, "What are we looking for?"

"We are looking for a liquor store. Not for the booze but for the gun they have behind the counter." We got there, and there was no one, not a single soul. The store looked untouched. I tried to open the door, but it was locked. I picked up a brick and broke the glass. The alarm went off. It was loud. I unlocked the door and went in. I found a 12-gauge shotgun and box of ammo. I looked around to turn off the alarm. But I couldn't find it. Carly screamed, and when I looked, I saw all the zombies coming. I grabbed two bottles of the moonshine and smashed them. I grabbed the box of matches I found on the shelf, and I set the store on fire. We went out the back door and went across the street to a store with a ladder going to the roof. We made it up the roof, and we lay down. The zombies didn't see or hear us, so we were good. I crawled over to the edge, and I looked over. I couldn't believe how many zombies were there. It was crazy. Carly looked like she wanted to cry, but she didn't. I told her they should be gone by tomorrow. We could sleep up here for the night. A few hours later, the bar was done burning; and we tried to get some sleep, but all the moaning kept us awake.

The next morning, Carly tapped me on the shoulder. I guess I fell asleep. She said, "They're all gone, but there are men down there talking." I got up and crawled over to the edge of the roof. When I got there, I saw three guys all with big guns and a truck. I asked Carly, "What should we do? Should we kill them or be friends with them?" She looked at me and said, "Let me introduce myself and see if they're friendly. If they try to hurt me, shoot them." I had no other plan, so that's what we did.

# Chapter 8

# THE MEN

The way Carly got the men's attention was kinda funny. She skipped singing to them. The men looked at her and started talking to her. I couldn't hear all that much about what they were talking about. But she waved at me to come over, so I got down from the roof and walked over to them. They took my guns and then patted me down. I thought was going to lose my guns, but they gave them back to me. One guy started to talk, saying, "Hello, I'm Mark. This is Sam, and that's Aaron. What are your names, guys?"

I said, "Hello, I'm Denver, and you guys already met Carly."

Then Mark asked, "Where are you guys from?"

I told them, "We came from a cabin out in the woods, but it burned down. Then we made our way here trying to get out of the way of that massive horde of zombies."

"Yeah, sorry about that," Aaron said.

"What are you sorry for?" I asked.

And he replied, "Well, you see, they were heading for our community, and we had to redirect them away, and it looks like they went right for you guys."

Carly and I looked at each other, and she then said, "You guys have a community?"

They were hesitant to say where, then Mark said, "Yeah, we do. Would you guys like to see it for yourselves?"

We both said yes, we would love to.

"We need to finish our run. Would you like to help?" So we did. When we got done, we headed to the community. It was a few miles from the cabin. When we got there, the gates opened, and I saw the most beautiful young lady. *I think I'm in love.* We got out of the truck, and she said hello. I blinked a few times and said, "Hello, I'm Denver, and this is Carly."

"Well, hello, I'm Emma, I'm kinda the leader here."

I asked, "Where exactly?"

Emma said, "Welcome to Refind. We take people in so we can help refine our lost world. Before we do anything, we have to do a welcome interview with the both of you. You know, just to ask some important questions and to see what you can bring to help us out."

"That's very smart," I said.

She took me into the house, and she turned on the lights. I froze in place. "The house still has power?"

Emma said, "Yeah, we have a nice, fast-moving river that one of our guys built for us."

"I thought I wouldn't see electricity ever again."

She chuckled and said, "Well, after our interview, you can take a nice hot shower."

"You have hot water?"

She smiled and said, "Yes, silly, we have hot water."

I smiled and we started the interview. She asked how many zombies I had killed. I told her a ton. I lost count. Then she asked me a weird question. "How many people have you killed?"

I looked at her and said, "I'm not a killer."

She smiled and then she said, "What can you bring to help us out?"

I told her about Frank and his guns. That he buried them somewhere on his property. She asked if I could show them where to go tomorrow. I didn't really want to go back out there, but she said she was going too; so of course, I said, "Yes, I'll show and help you find them."

After the interview, she took me back outside and asked Carly to come in to do her interview. Mark walked over to me, and he said he had to take my guns. I asked why. Mark said, "We have an armory here, so your guns will be safe. It's also because gunshots draw more of them. We are allowed to carry knives. Do you have one?"

I thought about it and said, "Okay, Mark, I trust you guys." I gave up my guns, and he asked again, "Do you have a pocket knife?" I felt my pockets and said, "No, I don't." He was super nice about it. He pulled out a knife out of his pocket and gave it to me. It was a beautiful knife. He said, "Here, you can have mine. I have a ton of knives. I was a collector when I was younger."

I waited until Carly was done with her interview. When Emma opened the door, she walked over to me and gave me a hug. I hugged her back, and she said, "Thank you for saving Carly. I was also lost when I was younger, and no one helped me. I'm glad there are still good people in this world."

Mark walked over to where Emma and I were, and Emma told him to show us to our house.

# CHAPTER 9

# THE HOUSE

Sam took us to the house and said, "You can use it." So the first thing I did was I took a hot shower. When I got out of the shower, I thought about putting the clothing I had back on, but then I saw a nice white robe, so I put that on, and I went to the bedroom. Carly was in the room across the hall, about to take a shower, so I knew that was her room now. I got in the room and looked around. It was a nice little room, like my apartment. I opened the drawer, and I saw many different clothing men's and women's, all sizes, so I put on some new clothing, and I felt amazing. A few moments later, there was a knock on the door, so I went downstairs and opened it. It was Emma. She said I looked good, and I blushed a little.

"Thank you. Thank you for taking us in, we really appreciate it." She smiled and asked me to follow her. I yelled upstairs, "Carly, I'll be back!" And we left.

We walked around the community, meeting everyone. It was beautiful. They had farm animals, horses and donkeys—they had like a whole zoo there. When we made it back to the house, she asked if Carly and I would love to have dinner with her. I said, "I would love to have dinner with you." She smiled and walked away. I told Carly about dinner, and she was happy because we haven't had a hot meal in a few days. Later that night, Carly and I went to Emma's house. I knocked on her door and she opened it. The whole house smelled so good. She invited us in, and we sat down at the table. She brought out a plate full of food. You should have seen Carly's eyes lit up like a Christmas tree. We ate a can of ham and veggies, and it was so good. We had a very good meal and conversations. I found out that

Carly was a runaway from a foster family that abused her. Emma—she's single and my age. We finished the night, and Emma reminded me about going to find the guns at Frank's tomorrow morning. Carly and I went back to the house, and we fell asleep.

# CHAPTER 10

# FRANK'S CABIN

When I woke up, I was fully refreshed. I haven't slept that well in a long time. I got ready for the day when there was a knock on the door. I went downstairs, and I saw Emma and a few men.

"Whenever you're ready, Denver, just come out, and we'll go," Emma said. I went back upstairs, and I told Carly, "I'll be back and stay safe." Then I left. We got in an older-looking car that one of the men brought here. Still had a full tank of gas. We went to Frank's cabin, and it was still smoking a little bit. I told them, "Frank buried them somewhere here on the property, so partner up and watch each other's backs and look for fresh dirt—that is where he buried the guns."

Everyone went their own ways, leaving me and Emma to be partners. We walked and walked around the property when Emma found it. She radioed everyone to help dig it up. When they all got there, it took five minutes to dig it up. One of the men jumped into the hole, hurting his foot, but he said he would be okay. He passed up the bag of guns. Emma opened it and saw all the guns and ammo. She smiled and almost cried. She jumped up and gave me a massive hug. Of course I hugged her back. Well, the guys were loading the guns in the truck. Emma and I went to the cabin, but there was nothing worth saving. Then I tripped over something. It was a thing of canned food. I picked it up, and the label was burned off, but I think the food inside was still good. Emma picked up one too then another and another. We both found twenty-four cans of food. We smiled, and when we looked up, we saw Mark and the others running to us like they were scared. We looked behind us and noticed a few zombies ten feet from us. We ran to the truck putting, the cans away, and returning to the others fighting the zombies. One of the men tripped and fell, but he got back up, but a zombie bit his arm. He screamed, and he killed the zombie. I ran over to him and grabbed one of the guys' machetes. I took one swing and cut his arm completely off. I took off my shirt and wrapped it around his hand. While I was doing that, the rest of them killed the last of the zombies. I yelled and told them, "We have to go right now!" I hurried and took off my belt and tied it tight around his arm and he passed out. A few of the men helped me pick him up, and we took him to the truck. We bolted out of there, making it back to Refind.

Emma radioed the community, telling the doctor to get ready. The gates opened, and we came to a sudden stop. We rushed him to the doctor, and he worked his magic on him. Emma and I went back to the armory where they were getting done unloading the guns and ammo. Emma introduced me to the keeper of their guns. She said, "Mario, this is Denver. He's the one who knew about all the guns and ammo."

"How many did we end up getting?" I asked him.

Mario said, "A lot. You brought us twenty-nine long guns and over thirty pistols and thousands of rounds of ammo. I'm still doing inventory on them."

Emma hugged and then kissed me. I was shocked that she did that. I went home to see how Carly was doing, and she was gone. I walked around, and I found her working on a garden, laughing with a few others around her age. I thought I'd leave her be. Emma came and got me to go check in on Scott. I asked, "Who's Scott?"

She said, "The one you cut off the hand. The doctor said he's done doing what he can."

When we got to the doctor's office, I saw Scott on the bed, sleeping.

"Is he going to be okay, Doctor?"

"Yes, he's going to be just fine. Whoever cut his hand off and applied the tourniquet saved his life."

"That would be me."

He looked at me. "Oh, a new face. What's your name, son?"

"I'm Denver."

"Hello, Denver, I'm Dr. Shu. You, sir, you saved Mr. Scott. His family is going to love you forever."

Emma and I went our own ways for the night.

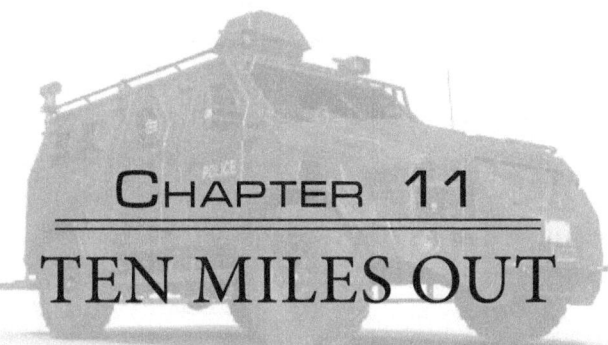

# CHAPTER 11

# TEN MILES OUT

The next morning, I woke up early. I had a bad feeling, but I was not sick. I just felt like something bad was going to happen. I went outside and started to walk the wall when I heard a weird noise. I climbed up the wall and saw a very large horde of zombies heading right for us. I fell down the wall in a hurry. I ran as fast as I could and went straight to Emma's house. I banged on her door, and she ran down in her underwear. I told her, "There's a massive horde coming from the back. We need to stop them before they break through the wall."

She ran to her room and raised everyone to get up and help. She got dressed and made it back to me with keys. We went outside to find people gathering in front of Emma's house. I started yelling at everyone who can shoot to get a gun. "Those who can drive, drive the cars to the south side of the wall. Protect the wall at all costs."

They all just stood there. Emma shouted, "You heard the man! Now go!" Everyone ran and did their jobs. We got the cars to the wall, but the horde was there before the people could retreat. Emma threw me the keys to a SWAT truck. She told me to turn on the sirens and honk the horn to get them away from here. I ran as fast as I could. I got to the truck, and I drove out and around. I turned on the sirens and honked the horn. It was extremely loud, which was good. They all started to turn toward me and follow me. I looked down at the gas tank, and I had less than half a tank of gas. I made it a mile away from Refind when Emma radioed me, saying, "You did it, they're all on you now. We're all safe, no one got hurt." I knew I couldn't just turn around, so I kept driving. I made it nine more miles when the truck started to cough, so I turned off the sirens, and then the truck stalled. I looked out the window, and they were still coming, so I locked the doors and hunkered down. I lay down on the bench in the back wall as the zombies moved past me. *Bang! Bang!* They were hitting the back and sides of the truck. What felt like forever was forever. I fell asleep in the back of the truck. When I woke up, I tried to radio Emma, but I was out of range. I looked around the truck and found a hidden compartment with a 9 mm in it. I dropped the mag to see five rounds and one in the chamber. I also found a grenade. I thought to myself that I could do it.

# Chapter 12

# ON MY WAY HOME

I was ten miles away from Refined and Emma. I love her. I have to make it back to her. If I walk three miles an hour, I could make it before dinner. I hoped they were out looking for me. I started my journey back home.

I was walking when I saw what looked like a family walking toward me. I still had my AR, but I used most of the rounds on many zombies before. But I remembered that I had the gun I found in that truck. They got closer, and I raised my AR.

"That's far enough. Where are you coming from and how many are there of you guys?"

The man said, "I'm Chris. Please don't shoot. I'm with my wife, Scarlet, and my two boys, Mitch and Robert. We're just passing through."

I repeated myself, "Where are you coming from?"

Chris said, "From the next town over, but it was overrun with the nonliving. Where are you coming from?"

I didn't want to tell them about Refind just yet because I didn't trust them at that moment. So all I said was "I'm just out here walking. Trying to find a place to stay." I lowered my gun, and they kept walking, and we went our own ways. I walked, and I was getting thirsty and hungry. I saw a small house down the road, so I decided to take a small break and go to the house. I hoped there's food in there. I got to the house and knocked on the door. But nobody answered the door. I opened the door, and the house stunk really bad, like really bad. I cleared the house and found a rotting body in the bathroom. He cut his arms to end his life. I opened the window and shut the door. I looked in the kitchen and found one can of dog food and a small opened bottle of water. I opened the front door and saw more zombies like a ton. I slowly closed the door and pulled the couch to block the door. *Welp! I'm stuck here now till they pass.* I opened the can of dog food and ate it. It wasn't all that bad. I peeked outside, and the sun was going down. When I was clearing the house, I saw a kid's room. The room had a small pink bear. I put it in my pocket, and I saw a nice brown bear that I would use for a pillow. I fell asleep on the couch. The next morning, I heard a truck driving by. I saw it when I looked out the window, and it was the truck that brought me and Carly to Refind. I hurried and grabbed my things and went outside. The truck slammed on its breaks, and Emma came out. She ran into my arms, crying. I pulled out the bear and gave it to her. She smiled more, and I kissed her. She didn't pull away, she kissed me back. When we stopped kissing, she said, "Let's go home."

# CHAPTER 13

# LOVE

We made it back to Refind, and I saw everyone. We parked the car, and when I got out, they all clapped and cheered for me. I looked at Emma. I then asked her, "What's going on and why are they clapping?"

She said, "You're our hero—you're my hero. You saved all of us."

That day, everyone was hugging me, and it felt weird. But I kinda liked it. I have never been loved like this before. I didn't know if they would leave me alone, but eventually, they did.

I went over to Emma's house, and she gave me the best night ever. That next morning, I went back to my house to check on Carly and found she was gone. I freaked out a little bit, and I went to go search for her. I ended up at the back of the store, and that's where I found her. She was in the garden, laughing and giggling with two other girls about her age. I was relieved that nothing bad happened to her.

I walked over to them, and they said, "Good morning, Mr. Denver."

"Well, good morning, ladies, I hope you guys are having a wonderful day." I went back over to Emma's house, and she was super happy to see me. She asked me if I would like to help her do some things. I said, "I would love to help you."

She took me around the back of Refind. There were a ton of zombie bodies back there just crawling around.

"We have to clean up the back wall and reinforce it." So we started cleaning and burning all the bodies. Some of the men came out with some steel sheets and some rebar to help rebuild the wall. When we were done, Emma took me to where we got our running water from. We used the truck that was on the south side of the wall. We drove about a mile away to a massive query. It was full of beautiful blue water with a large fence around it. I asked if anyone else knew about it, and she said just a few people. We took turns driving around and making sure the fence was all intact and that there were no zombies in the water. We have a water filter as well. We have to change it every few months. We got done driving around, and Emma took me back to her house. We spent the rest of the night talking. We talked about our childhood and where we grew up. Came to find out we went to the same school and even had a few of the same teachers. Wow, it's such a small world.

Our night ended with me and Emma in bed. She looked at me and said, "Denver, I think I'm in love with you."

I looked at her, and without hesitation, I said, "I love you too. You make me the happiest guy in the world. Well, what's left of the world anyways."

# Chapter 14

# MORE PEOPLE

The next morning, I woke up and looked at Emma. She was still sleeping, and she looked super cute. I slowly got up and went downstairs. I looked in the cupboards to make her something for breakfast. She had a pancake mix, so it looks like I'm making her pancakes. When I got done making them, I felt so good. I looked in the fridge and cut a small pat off the butter. She didn't have any syrup, so I hope she'd like them. When I went back upstairs, I woke her up super nicely. When she woke up, she had a massive smile.

"You made me breakfast? No one has ever made me breakfast in bed before."

A knock on the door interrupted us. I told Emma I'd get the door. I walked downstairs and opened the door. There were like fifteen new people. I went back up the stairs and Emma finished her pancakes. I told her about the newcomers, and when she came downstairs, she was super happy she even asked me if I would like to do some of the interviews to make it go faster.

"I would love to help you," I said to her.

It took us two hours to complete the interviews. When we got done, Sam took them to their new house, and they loved it so much. I met back up with Emma, and we discussed the interviews. She told me that the kids were taken from an orphanage by the workers. They didn't have anything to bring to Refind. She looked a little bummed out. But I cheered her up by saying, "They did bring something to Refind—they brought themselves. We can use them for watchers and someone to do yard work."

She smiled and said, "You're right, we *can* use them."

Sam came back with one of the kids and said the kid had something to say that I thought was a good idea. "Well, what's your idea?"

"My name is Timmy."

"Well, hello, Timmy, I'm Denver, and you already met Emma. So what's the big idea?" Timmy went on to tell us that on the way here, he saw a farm with a few horses, and he thought he saw some other animals there as well. Timmy then said he was thinking that maybe we could go and gather them up and bring them here. I thought about it, and it was a cool idea, but we would have to build a pen for them. Timmy said he would build it if he knew how.

Sam said, "You know what? I'll help you build it, and I'll teach you the ropes around here." Emma and I smiled, and we went to round up and to talk to some of our people. We decided to go where Timmy said the farm was. When we got there, we saw some horses, pigs, and cows. There were a few zombies about to break open the gate, so we knew we had gotten there just in time. We ran and came up from behind them and stabbed them in the back of the head. We had no idea how we were going to take the animals back to Refind.

I walked around the farm and saw a truck and a large trailer that can carry all if not most of them. I looked in the truck, and there was a dead person in the driver's seat. When I opened the door, I found out that it was a zombie, and then it tried to bite me. I was so close to being bit by it. I grabbed my knife and stabbed it in the head. It fell flat on the steering wheel. I dragged it out of the truck, and it fell to the ground. I looked in the truck, and it was the only one there. I hopped in the truck, and the keys were in the ignition. I turned the key, and the truck started. I pulled to the back, and Emma and the gang had their guns drawn on me. I stopped the truck and opened the door and said, "Don't shoot! It's me, Denver." It took about five hours to gather all the animals and put them in the trailer.

"I hope they finished the pen for the animals before we get back," I said. We also found a few chickens and roosters so we can have fresh eggs. We made our way back to Refind, and when we got there, the gates opened. I saw the most beautiful pen ever. All the kids were helping and were cheering and laughing. We unloaded the animals in the pen, and it was just so amazing. We don't know how long they will last, but we were going to try to breed them so we could have food for as long as possible.

## CHAPTER 15

# THE WATER

It was early morning when I woke up after I heard a noise outside. I went to check it out, and when I went downstairs, I looked outside, and there was a black-and-yellow cat. I decided to leave it be because it wasn't hurting anyone. But, man, was I thirsty. So I went to the kitchen, and I turned on the water. It was bloody. I dumped out the bloody water in the sink. I hurried to Emma and told her about the water. She got up and got ready for the day and called everyone on the walkie-talkie to not use the water.

Emma and I went to check out the pond, and there were dead zombies all over and in the pond. Someone killed them and dumped them there. She got super angry and was about to storm off, but I hugged her. "Emma, we'll figure out who did this and I'll get some guys to help clean the pond up."

We went back to Refind to gather some friends to help us clean. Jacob came from the front gate worried; he went right up to us. I was talking to Emma when he interrupted us.

"They left, the new folks they left like three hours ago. They told me to open the gates because they were coming. I didn't know what they meant, so I let them out."

Emma replied, "Well, if they want to leave, let them leave. I can only help the ones who stay. Did they take anything with them?"

Jacob said, "They took some food, but not really anything else."

I butted in, saying, "We need some people to help clean the pond where we get our drinking water. Do you think you can round up some to help?"

"Yeah, I can," he replied. We got a few more folks, and we went back to the pond. One after another, we pulled out zombies. Frankie, one of our night watchers, pulled out a body with a note in a bottle. He yelled to me, "Hey, I have something over here!"

I rushed to him, not knowing what he had. And when I got there, he opened it and said, "We're watching you! Stay out of our land!"

When we got done with the pond, we cleaned the filter and headed back to Refind. When we got there, I told Emma we needed to double the watch at least for a few days. She agreed. I looked over, and I saw the family that left this morning talking to Jacob. I walked over and asked, "What happened? Why did you leave?"

Pill, who was the father, said, "I had a dream that the fire burned down and all my kids died in that fire. I had to take my family and leave for our safety. I'm sorry if I scared anyone."

"You're good, Pill. Next time, please say something less scary."

We went the rest of the night taking care of the animals.

# Chapter 16
# THE HELICOPTER

We left Refind on lockdown for a week after we found the note in the bottle. We only let people out to get things like gas, if there's any, and the important things we need. Carly came over to Emma's house and said she saw a helicopter land in the distance. I thought it was a good idea, but Emma didn't. She said, "We don't want to risk the attention of the people who wrote the note. We don't want to start a war."

Carly looked at me, and I whispered, "I'll try to get her to agree."

I talked to Emma about the helicopter and how if we had it how scary we could be. "Do you think the people will mess with us if we have a helicopter?"

She paused and said, "Do you even know how to fly a helicopter??"

I said, "Yeah, I do."

After a little while, she agreed and said, "Go in the morning and take Donny with you."

The next day, I went to see Carly so she could point me in the right direction.

She said, "No, I'm coming with you guys."

I didn't want her to go, but it's been a while since she's been outside of the walls, so she needed to stay sharp just in case anything happens to Refind. So we got some supplies and left. During our way, Carly asked if I knew how to fly a helicopter, just in case we wanted to take it home with us.

I said, "Yeah, I know. I used to play a helicopter simulator game when I was younger, how difficult can it be?"

Donny looked at me puzzled and said, "So you don't really know how to fly it?"

"Well, I always wanted to become a helicopter pilot, but I never had the money, so I just watched a ton of YouTube videos on it. We found the helicopter, and it was at a small military base. But the bad news was there were hundreds of zombies inside the fence. The good news was we found the helicopter; it was a beautiful Black Hawk helicopter. The helicopter had .50 caliber guns on both sides. But there were no keys in it. There was a small building as well, but I'm guessing that was full of zombies too. We looked around the base to see if we could find an opening, and sure enough, there was a big fence gate locked. I saw a zombie in a pilot uniform, so hopefully, he had the keys to the helicopter.

So what we did was we got poles, and we banged on the fence and started to stab them in the eyes to the brain. One after another, we killed all the ones outside. I pulled the car around and drove through the gate opening. I got out of the car and went to the pilot. He had the keys in his pocket and a beautiful gun, but no ammo. Carly and Donny went to the building and looked in the windows. They saw tons more zombies inside. They thought it was over because soon as we opened the door, they were all going to flee out all at once. I went over to them and made a plan.

"Carly, you open the door, and as soon as one comes out, close it. Donny and I will kill them when they come out."

We got into place, and one after the other, we killed them. But out of nowhere, Carly couldn't hold the door anymore. The door swung open, letting out the rest of the zombies.

"RUN, CARLY, RUN!"

Carly took off running. Donny and I retreated as well. We were toast. The car was inside the gate, and there was no way we could take them all. I looked over to the helicopter and ran to it. I yelled at Donny and Carly to get down. I jumped on to the .50 caliber and started shooting—*bang, bang, bang*—over and over, and they all dropped like flies. I had the keys to the helicopter, so I started it up and it had a full tank of gas. I left it running and went back to the building and opened the door and knocked to make sure that there were no more zombies in there. I walked in and saw tons of meals ready to eat, also known as MREs. We just hit the jackpot.

Donny and Carly started to load them into the car and some into the helicopter because one way or another, I was taking that home with me. I continued to search the base and found a small locked room. I grabbed a crowbar that was lying outside the room and tried to open it. Took all my might, but I soon got it open. It was full of guns and more MREs. I started to load them up into the helicopter and car. We got almost done when a gunshot went off, and Donny fell to the ground. I pulled my gun and shot. A man fell to the ground, and Carly shot him in the head. We ran over to Donny, but he was already gone too. I grabbed my knife and gently stabbed him in the head.

*Jeremiah Breuer*

# Chapter 17

# WHAT DO WE DO NOW?

Carly started to cry and went over to Donny's body. A strong voice said, "Don't move or I'll shoot."

I looked up from Carly and saw a guy holding a shotgun pointed at me. I put my hands in the air, then a gun went off. I closed my eyes thinking I got shot, but I didn't feel any pain. I opened my eyes, and that guy was dead on the ground. I looked around, wondering who killed him. I looked down at Carly, and she had a smoking gun in her hand. She just saved my life. I was in disbelief and shock. I looked back at her and gave her the biggest hug and said, "Let's get out of here." She asked if she could drive the car back, and I tried to take the helicopter back. I said yeah, so I showed her how to drive, and she was a natural.

I grabbed Donny's body and laid him in the back of the back so we could have a proper burial for him. I got in the helicopter, and it was ready for takeoff. I did a made-up checklist and flipped the switches and moved the handle back, and the helicopter lifted into the air. I went up about four hundred feet and started making my way back to Refind. I was going slow enough for Carly. I looked down to the ground and saw her driving home. I waited till she got there to land. I slowly started to land, and when I touched the ground, I turned off the engine.

Emma came out and saw Donny. She ran over to him and saw he was dead. "What happened?"

I started to explain everything, and then when I told her about Carly saving my life, she teared up and gave her a big hug. "Thank you for saving

Denver. I was worried about you guys." Emma looked around and saw all the MREs and gasped that we had enough food to last a long time. I also showed her the guns we found, and she was so happy.

I looked at Carly, and she looked at me, and I said to her, "Watch this." I pulled a fat diamond ring I found on a zombie and got down on one knee. "Emma, while I was gone, I could not stop thinking about you. When I first met you, I fell in love. I knew you were the one. Will you do me the honor and become my wife?"

She cried, saying, "YES!"

We unloaded the car and helicopter and put everything away where it goes. Everyone came to the front because they heard the helicopter. When they saw it, they were scared until they realized it was me who brought it there. They saw the ring on Emma, and they congratulated us on it.

# CHAPTER 18

# ONE YEAR LATER

Emma and I were extremely happy together, but it's not just us anymore. Yup, you guessed it: Emma's pregnant. We don't have the tools to know the gender, but it's okay, we like the surprise. We don't have much baby stuff, so we need to go get some supplies. We still have a ton of MREs to last for a while.

More good news: our cattle tripled over the year. We had to expand the pen. Now the whole back side of Refind is a massive pen. We were thinking about expanding Refind out more to build more houses. We also have a five-man crew. They go out and gather supplies whenever we needed them. They couldn't get any baby things. So I have decided to go out and get the things myself. I know a place by my house—I mean my old house where I used to live before all this.

Over the last year, we got an older man who knew how to fly a helicopter. He showed me how to work everything and how to fly it. I talked to Emma, and she said it was okay for me to go. I packed a bag of food, and when I was getting ready to leave, Carly came out of nowhere and tossed her bag in the helicopter. I was going to tell her no, but she left. I didn't think about it much until she came back with a shopping cart full of gas cans. She told me she siphoned the last of the gas in all the diesel trucks. I thought about it and told her, "Yeah, let's go."

We started to take off, and I thought I should apologize to Carly. "Hey, Carly…"

She looked at me and she said, "What?"

"I'm sorry I didn't look for your family."

She smiled and told me, "It's okay, Denver. I was left at a firehouse by my parents, and I went to a foster home and another and so many more, and I got sick of it so I ran away. But it's okay now, Denver. You're my family now."

I felt so much better knowing she's okay. We made it so close to my old town, and I saw a ton of zombies. It was insane how many there were. I landed the helicopter about a half mile from the baby place. We landed on a small building, but the helicopter sound made it where a horde of zombies were coming our way. We knew it would happen, but we didn't know there would be so many. We locked the helicopter up and hunkered down. What we thought was a ton of zombies was a lot of zombies. But I was glad we landed over here because the zombies didn't know where the sound came from. They just kept walking past us like we were never there. It took about seven hours for all the zombies to walk past us. We left and went to the baby store. I tried to open the front door, but it was locked. "I know another way," I told Carly. "There's an air vent in the back, and I think we can pop it open and see if we can get the door open." I popped it and waited—no noise, so I knew there was no one in there. I crawled in and opened the door. There was no alarm, so we were good. Just to be safe, we cleared the building. I went to the baby cribs, and Carly went to the baby food to see if there was anything we could salvage, but there was nothing left that was still good. We didn't get many baby things, but we did get a crib, so we decided to go back to the helicopter.

When we got back, Carly put some things in the helicopter. I turned my back for one second to pick something off the ground when I heard Carly scream. I looked, and there were two men holding Carly down. I pulled out my gun and shot the man holding her down. Blood and brains went everywhere. The other man raised his gun and—*bang*!—I shot him, and down he went. Then all of a sudden, everything went red then black.

# CHAPTER 19

# AM I DEAD?

I couldn't see anything; everything was black. I felt like I was moving and I could feel my body shaking. I was trying to hear, but all I heard was a pinging sound. *Man, my head hurts really bad.* I felt a little bit in my hands. I moved, and I could feel the grass and rocks; then I didn't feel anything at all. Then I felt a sharp pain in my arm going up to my head, then everything stopped hurting. I had no pain. I only saw Emma and I smiled, but my lips didn't move. After what seemed like forever, I could finally see. I saw a light, and I was walking to it. When I got to the light, it vanished, and I could hear Emma's voice.

"You can do it, Denver, I love you."

I started to fight the darkness and make my way to her voice. That was the only thing keeping me going. Her voice was slowly fading, then it got louder and louder. Finally, I could see her; she was crying. I looked around, and I could see almost everyone that lived at Refind.

"We are all here, Denver," Emma said.

I could only see out of my right eye. My head hurt really bad.

"What happened?"

Emma said to me with tears in her eyes, "You've been shot, Denver, but you're going to be okay. The bullet grazed past your head, nicking your eye socket." Emma held up a small mirror. I looked, and I didn't recognize the guy looking back at me. My face was black and blue with blood all over.

"Emma? I love you so much, your voice was the only thing I heard, and I followed it back to you."

She started to cry, and she came in and gave me a hug and a kiss.

I looked over at Carly. "Thank you for getting me home."

She smiled at me. "You're welcome. I saw how you fly it but not really how you land it, but I got you here. I crashed and landed it. I'm sorry, Denver, it won't fly anymore."

"I don't care about the helicopter. I care about you. Are you okay? Did you get hurt?"

She looked down, and I saw her ankle.

"I just sprained my ankle, that's all," she said.

"I'm thankful you're okay."

# Chapter 20
# HEALING TAKES TIME

It had been two weeks since I was shot. And my head still hurt, but not really that bad. I was so glad we have a doctor at Refind. Because if we didn't, I sure enough would be dead.

I went back to the med house for a checkup. Dr. Dan took off my bandage, and I could see a little blurry, but I could see. The doc told me that everything was looking great. I should be healed in a few more weeks. He cleaned me up and put new bandages on my head and gave me some meds that we have left. I left the med house and went to the front gate to see the helicopter because I really just stayed in bed for the last two weeks. When I got to the front gate, a few people clapped and told me I was doing great. I saw the helicopter outside the gate. The tail of the helicopter was bent, and the rotors were broken, but it was okay. I was not mad. I was just glad Carly knew how to fly it and get me home safely.

All of a sudden, I heard Emma shouting, "Everyone, stay indoors, and the ones who are outside, come get a gun. We have a breach!"

I turned to the armory and ran. I grabbed a gun and went to the back wall. I killed a few zombies, and I saw a few people with knives killing some too. I saw a zombie about to bite Jerry. I shouted, "Jerry, look out!" I shot the zombie. Jerry dropped and got back up, and I tossed him my gun. He killed more zombies, and we patched the hole in the back of the gate.

Emma was there and saw that the hole was created by someone from inside. "Looks like someone wanted to leave without anyone knowing, but why not go through the front gate?"

I didn't have an answer for her. We cleared Refind, making sure none got through us. We went back to the wall to see what we lost. We lost six good men and women fighting for Refind. Emma didn't know what to do. She started to break down, so I jumped in.

"Okay, everyone, let's take the bodies and burn them, and let's bury our loved ones and give them a proper goodbye." After we buried our dead, we had a few people wanting to leave because they felt that Refind was unsafe. But really, everywhere was unsafe these days.

"If you guys want to leave, you may. But starting tomorrow, I will be giving a shooting class." Emma looked at me, and I said, "Whoever can shoot will be given a gun if they are eighteen or older."

I looked back at Emma, and she said, "If you stay, we promise you we will be safe."

Most of the people who wanted to leave decided to stay, but we did have a family leave.

"All right, everyone, I'll see you in the morning. Good night."

We all went our separate ways. I went inside with Emma, and I was expecting her to yell at me about telling everyone that they could carry, but she wasn't mad. She told me it was a great idea to teach just in case it happens again or we have to deal with some bad people.

# Chapter 21
# LEARNING TO SHOOT

Emma and I woke up, expecting more people to leave, but the rest all stayed. I went outside, and there was a line at the armory. I walked over to the armory, and I started to pass out guns to those who wanted it. I also showed a few people how to hold the gun and how to shoot.

Emma came outside and gave a small speech about them making Refind a better place and to remind them that these guns were for the last resort. I looked over at Emma; she was getting bigger every day. I really couldn't wait till the baby is born. She was about seven months pregnant. We were not exactly sure, but we thought it's been seven months. She also told the people that if they have any kids ages ten to seventeen, we have BB guns that we could train on; and if they respected these guns, they will be given a real one with the parents' permission, of course, and with my approval. I had a few parents come to me and Emma, and they asked if we could show their kids how to shoot.

We had seven kids. I gave each one of them BB guns, and we set up some cans for them to shoot. Four out of the seven didn't know how to hold or shoot, and the other three were pros. So we had them help with the younger ones. The three got real guns because I felt like they were responsible. Emma went back inside the house. While I was teaching the kids how to shoot, Carly came over and asked if she could carry her gun. I already knew she could shoot, so I said yes, and she went and got her gun. Eight weeks later, all the kids had real guns, and we had more people to keep watch as well.

We grew over the past eight weeks, and now we have more doctors. I was fully healed, and Emma and Carly were doing very well. We also have a professional butcher and a dairy farmer to milk our cows. We got a few people to go out hunting, and they came back with three deer. Emma was due anytime now, and she's been in a lot of pain.

One of our hunters came over and knocked on the door. When I opened the door, the lead hunter, Colton, handed me a bottle of painkillers and some deer meat. He also handed me some clean needles.

I asked him, "Why are you giving me needles?"

He smiled and gave me a vial of morphine for Emma. "I thought she might need it for the pain."

I thanked him, and then Emma screamed, "DENVER, MY WATER BROKE!"

I looked back at Colton, and he smiled. "Well, get in there, Dad, she needs you. I'll go get the doctor for you guys."

"Thank you, Colton." I turned and ran to Emma. I showed her the morphine, and she told me to give her twenty milligrams, so I did. She stopped screaming, so I knew it worked. Soon, the doctor came in, and helped with the child's birth.

# CHAPTER 22

# IT'S A...

It's been thirteen hours, and the baby was still not out yet. I was holding Emma's hand and she was pushing and pushing. And finally, a head popped out then the rest of the body. The baby started to cry, and Doctor Jay asked me if I wanted to cut the cord, so I grabbed the scissors and cut the cord. It was nasty but beautiful.

Doctor Jay took the baby and washed it off. He dried the baby off and wrapped it in a blanket. He turned and announced it was a beautiful baby girl and gave her to Emma. Emma was out of breath, but she was a fighter and she was going to be okay. I hugged Emma and the baby, and we came up with the name Anne. I went outside and told everyone.

"It's a baby girl, and her name is Anne! She's about six pounds and some ounces. Both Mom and Anne are doing well." Everyone cheered and congratulated us.

I went back inside and Emma said she was going to sleep. Doctor Jay told me he gave her some more morphine to ease her pain. Doctor Jay gave me baby Anne, and he said he'd be back to check up on them. I laid Anne in the crib and went to make Emma some dinner. I got dinner done, and a knock on the door almost woke them up. I slowly opened the door, and it was Carly. She came with a basket of fruit and a blender. I asked Carly if she would like some venison, and she said yes, she would like some.

"How do you want it cooked?"

She said, "Dead."

We both laughed just a little too loud, and we woke up Emma. She got up and slowly walked to the kitchen to see us cooking and enjoying a conversation. She said that the food smelled so good, so I made her a plate and poured her a glass of grape juice we had.

We ate dinner and a few more of the older people came by to see the baby and check in on us. At the end of the day we both got no sleep because Anne was up most of the night, crying.

# CHAPTER 23

# THE WORLD IS COMING BACK

One of our men here at Refind, Gary, is an inventor. He was able to make a radio and get it working. After doing that, it would only receive a broadcast from one station, the military broadcast station, saying that there was indeed a cure for what had happened to us. They were telling us that after the cure was administered, if you were to get bit or scratched, you would no longer turn into a zombie.

I thanked Gary for showing me the radio and how it was receiving messages from other places. I left Gary and went to tell Emma about the radio and what I had heard on the broadcast. When I got to our house, I found Emma feeding Anne. Excitedly, I told her all that I had heard on the radio. She smiled so big and said to me that we must find out where they were giving out this cure.

I agreed and told her that I would do my best to find the location of where this cure was being passed out. I left Emma and went back over to where Gary was. Sure enough, when I got there, Gary was still listening to the very same guy saying all the same stuff about the cure. The guy on the radio was telling us that the cure was being distributed in Washington DC. Unfortunately, we were currently in Texas. According to my calculations, that was about 1,500 miles away. There was *no* chance we could make it all that way. I wish that the helicopter was still in operational condition.

As I was leaving, the military guy said they would be doing air drops in different states. He named most of the states. Then he said something beautiful to my ears, "El Paso, Texas." Knowing this bit of information and that we were only shy of Dallas, I was even more excited. I continued to listen to the man on the radio to hear when the drop was going to be made in El Paso. He then said it would be dropped in three days' time. I left Gary to go back to tell Emma that I had found out the day the drop was to be made.

I told her that I wanted to help Refind to get the cure. She told me to ask if there were people who would join me in helping Refind get the cure.

I called for a town meeting. Everyone from Refind showed up for the meeting. I told the people that Gary had made a radio, and on that radio, we heard about the cure being air-dropped in many states, including Texas. I let them know that we also found that the closest city for a drop was going to be El Paso. Almost all at once, they started cheering. As I continued to tell them what I had learned, I let them know that the drop in El Paso was planned in just three days. I told them that I was definitely going to go. I then asked the people, "Who among you will join me on a trip to El Paso?"

There were several men who stood up, saying, "I'm going, to save my family." After people heard that statement, more people stood up, cheering and saying, "I'm going!"

"Yeah, me too!"

"And me!"

"I'll go!" another said.

Now I had to pick only four out of the group who stood up. These people would join me, and I would have to trust them—and they me—with our lives. Emma handed me a set of keys. She said, "Take my car. I parked it in the garage when this whole thing started."

The guys and I were getting ready for our journey to El Paso. I walked over to the garage. As the door was opening, I noticed that the car was a Toyota Prius. As I got into the small little car, that's when I noticed that the gas tank was full and the battery gauge said that the battery was fully charged. "This is just enough to get us there and about a quarter of the way back." We would have to squeeze into the car two five-gallon jugs of gasoline that I had been saving. I figure that we would have to walk or find an alternative method of transportation for the remainder of the trip when the gas and battery run out. After pulling the car to the front gate, the guys all got into the car. With the guys and the two gas cans, it was a very tight fit, but we were able to close the doors without any problems.

Emma, holding Anne, leaned down to me as I rolled down my window. I gave her and Anne a big kiss, then we drove away.

# CHAPTER 24

# THE TRIP

After starting on our journey, we arrived at the expressway. On the side of the road was a street sign that read El Paso, 450 miles ahead. On our drive, several of the guys were sleeping while the others played small little games like "I spy," or finding different license plates on all the parked cars on the roads. As we drove on, we came to a section of the expressway where the road was totally demolished.

Turning around and trusting only paper maps we found in the glove compartment, since we had no electronic maps, Matt, who I call my navigator, had found a road running parallel to the expressway we were on. This side road would allow us to bypass the missing section we came across, therefore allowing us to get back onto the expressway. It took about seventeen miles on this side road, but we were able to make it back onto the expressway.

As we continued on our way, Alex, who was sitting right behind Matt, told us that some time ago, he lived in this area we were driving through and that he knew of a large store that once sold things like sporting goods and outdoor stuff, maybe even camping things. I did not plan on stopping, but the guys all took a vote and were in favor of stopping and looking to see if this place he told us was still there and still having stuff there. We got off at the next off-ramp and made our way to the place Alex told us about.

Arriving at the location, we found the parking lot *full* of cars. It was just like the store was open and having a 75 percent–off sale.

We found a parking spot right in front, so we parked and got out of the car. Looking around very carefully, we were able to peek into a store window, and what we saw was totally amazing. There in just one store were so many zombies. There were just too much for the five of us to handle.

We decided to walk back to the car. Walking back, we heard and then saw zombies coming toward us.

Making it back safely to the car, we hightailed it out of there, leaving them in our dust. I let Matt drive because I had already been driving for what seemed to be all day. Ahead of us, we could see that the weather was turning for the worse. The sky was not its beautiful blue anymore but a dark gray, nearly black, and lightning was starting to flash before our eyes.

Slowing the car down and bringing it to a stop, Matt asked us guys if we should continue through the upcoming weather or stop and find shelter for the night. I personally did not want to test the storm, but wanting to keep the guys in decision making, we voted on what to do next. Before we could vote, we kind of just decided to find shelter for a while and wait for the storm to pass. We pulled off the expressway and found a nearby hotel. This hotel seemed to be in perfect condition, looking good, and no signs of zombies anywhere near it.

Walking into the hotel, Matt being a jokester as he is, rang the front desk bell as to hail a bellboy or front desk agent.

To our surprise, a single zombie dressed like a bell boy came around the corner; and as quick as can be, Matt took his knife and killed him. I yelled out to Matt, "There is another one!" Matt quickly turned and stabbed the zombie right in the left eye. That zombie then dropped to the ground and stopped moving. As he hit the ground, a large set of keys fell from the pocket of the zombie. We separated the set of keys among ourselves to clear the hotel faster and to find a good room for us to stay in for a while. We went our separate ways for a few. about a half hour later, we met up in the lobby to talk about what the next move would be. We all showed up except one. Matt was gone. He never made it to the lobby. As we were pondering if Matt had fallen asleep or gotten hurt. We heard glass break, and we ran to help. We found Matt smiling as he was grabbing food and putting it into his pockets.

We all started to laugh and joined in. The soda machine next to the snack machine was our next target.

Nicky popped the lock that was locking the soda into the Machine. We drank soda and ate junk food as the storm was going by. We decided to all get rooms that were connected. I got into my room and used the couch to barricade the door. And then I jumped onto the bed and, in no time, fell asleep.

I woke up and found it was the next morning. Matt was knocking on my door, I moved the couch and let him in. Coming in, Matt opened the curtains and showed me all the destruction the storm had caused. I told Matt that I was sure glad we decided to stop. We both laughed and woke up all the others so we could continue on our way to El Paso.

After driving for some time, we made it to El Paso, but it was totally overrun by zombies. We had gotten there a whole day early. We made camp right outside what would be the drop site. Roughly about four hours went by, and we heard a plane in the area. It looked to be a military plane like a C-17 Globemaster. I told the guys that the plane was a day early. We watched as it parachuted a crate down to the earth. Jumping into the car, we drove right over to the drop site. The cure hit the ground, and immediately, it was surrounded by zombies.

As we pulled up to the crate's landing area, we saw many cars and trucks driving up as well. This told us that there were other survivors. We noticed a guy on a truck pulled out an RPG and shot it into a field. Hearing the shot, the zombies turned and ran toward the field and away from the crate.

Several of the people ran over to the crate. We stopped our vehicle and also ran toward the crate. To my surprise, they did not try to kill us but rather helped us because they knew there was plenty of the cure for everyone. We took five racks of fifty—that was 250 vials of the cure for everyone at Refind, including any newcomers if there were any. We five got back into the car, and everyone else left, going their own way.

# CHAPTER 25

# THE WAY HOME

The drive back home was going as good as it could go, but just as we were about a hundred miles or so from our destination, the car, having no more gas and now out of electricity, lost all power and was coming to a stop.

Looking at each other and knowing that this was bound to happen, we all started to laugh. The three in the back seat were handing Matt some candy bars, I asked, "What were those for?" Matt told me that they had a bet on how far the car would make it, and I won. Matt then said, "They were a hundred miles off, and I was only seventy-five miles off." I laughed with them about the matter, and we got out of the car and began our long walk home. We walked for what seemed to be hours; it was getting dark out. We found a sleeper semitruck to hunker down in for the night.

The next morning, we were about to start our walk when Jack honked the semitrucks horn by accident. The semitruck's batteries were still good after about two years of sitting. Looking at Jack, I said to him , "There is no way."

Jack, seeing the key of the truck on the floor, quickly picked it up and placed it into the ignition and, turning the key, the light came on and the engine roared to life.

We all were bamboozled. Matt yelled from the driver's seat, "It's alive!"

All of us got back into the truck, and Matt started to drive the semi back to Refind. We did not expect to make it all the way back to Refind because we thought that the fuel in the tank was very old; but sure enough, we made it. We were home, and I got to see my beautiful girls.

The people from Refind all gathered around. We passed out the cure. Everyone now had their share.

"The zombies no longer know we are here and cannot hurt us anymore."

I went back to Gary's house, where the radio was. Gary had the radio powered on, and we heard the announcer say people were going to rise up and kill all the zombies so we could take our world back.

Emma told me that she wanted Anne to grow up in a zombie-free world. With this cure, I believe that it might just happen.

# CHAPTER 26

# NOW WE FIGHT

Six months later...

We were working on the extinction of the last of the zombies. Over the radio, we heard, "More and more towns and cities, and for that matter, entire states are now zombie free. The larger states still have some zombies roaming around, and we will need to concentrate our efforts on those states."

Emma and I were talking about going and living in a state that was already zombie free. She agreed about the move, and we then told all our friends here at Refind about our plans to move, most of the younger people sounded like they too would like to go, while the older people were set on staying put here in Refind.

We broke up into two groups. One group would be a group that would head out into the world and move to a state that was zombie free. While the other group would stay here in Refind and continue to build up Refind. There were about fifty of us set on going while only about seventy wanted to stay. Emma, at the last minute, decided she too wanted to stay for the baby's sake. Wanting the best for our small little family, I agreed we would stay. It was time for the group that was leaving to go through the gates for what would be the last time. We gave them all the guns and ammo they had when they first came to Refind. We also gave them plenty of food that should last them a few weeks.

Emma went back inside to feed Anne. I did the best I could to make a good life for myself, Emma, and little Anne and the entire Refind family.

Time marched on. Another six months had now gone by. The USA as a whole had now become zombie free. The military had grown every day for the last year, and it was a great feeling to just stand at home knowing I and my family are safe. Of course there still were cities and towns out there who still didn't trust the outside world, and I really couldn't say I blame them. There were communities like Refind who opened their gates for the families without a home to come live with them in peace.

Over the next few years, Refind had become one of the largest safe havens in all of Texas.

Living among us now, we have some military personnel and their families. Everyone was doing their part in keeping Refind a safe community. Emma and I were now expecting our second child. Anne is doing wonderful. Over the last couple of weeks, she had started to crawl. I know it's a cliché, but we actually are living happily ever after.

The End